For my three lovable shadows:
Hudson, Grace and Teddy.

This topsy-turvy turn around book lets you read one story and then turn the book around to read another.

Enjoy!

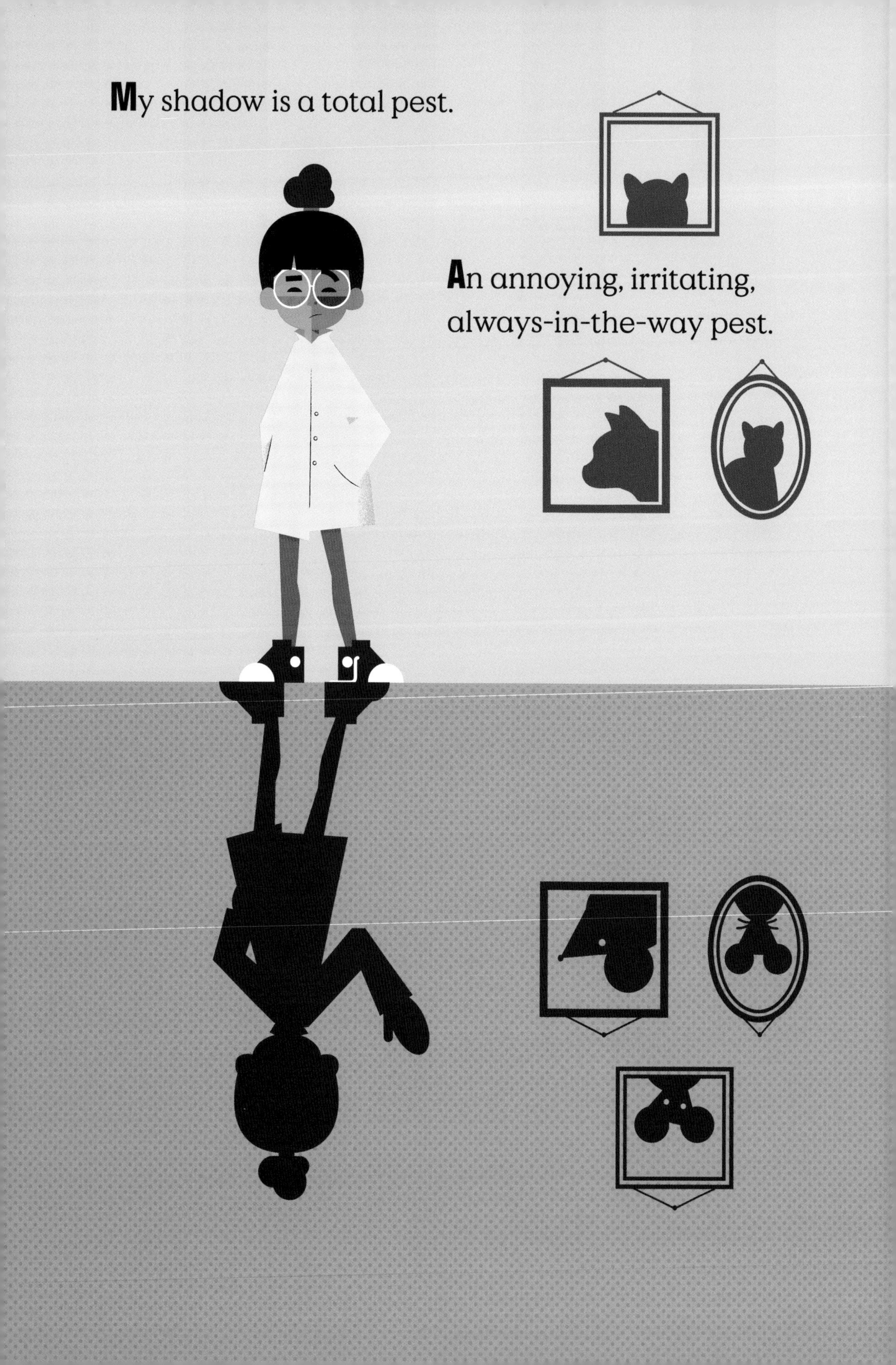

My shadow is a total pest.

An annoying, irritating, always-in-the-way pest.

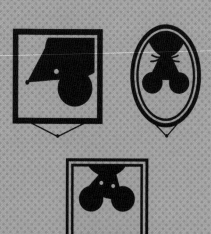

Because I get to spend all my days with you.

But it sure is great.

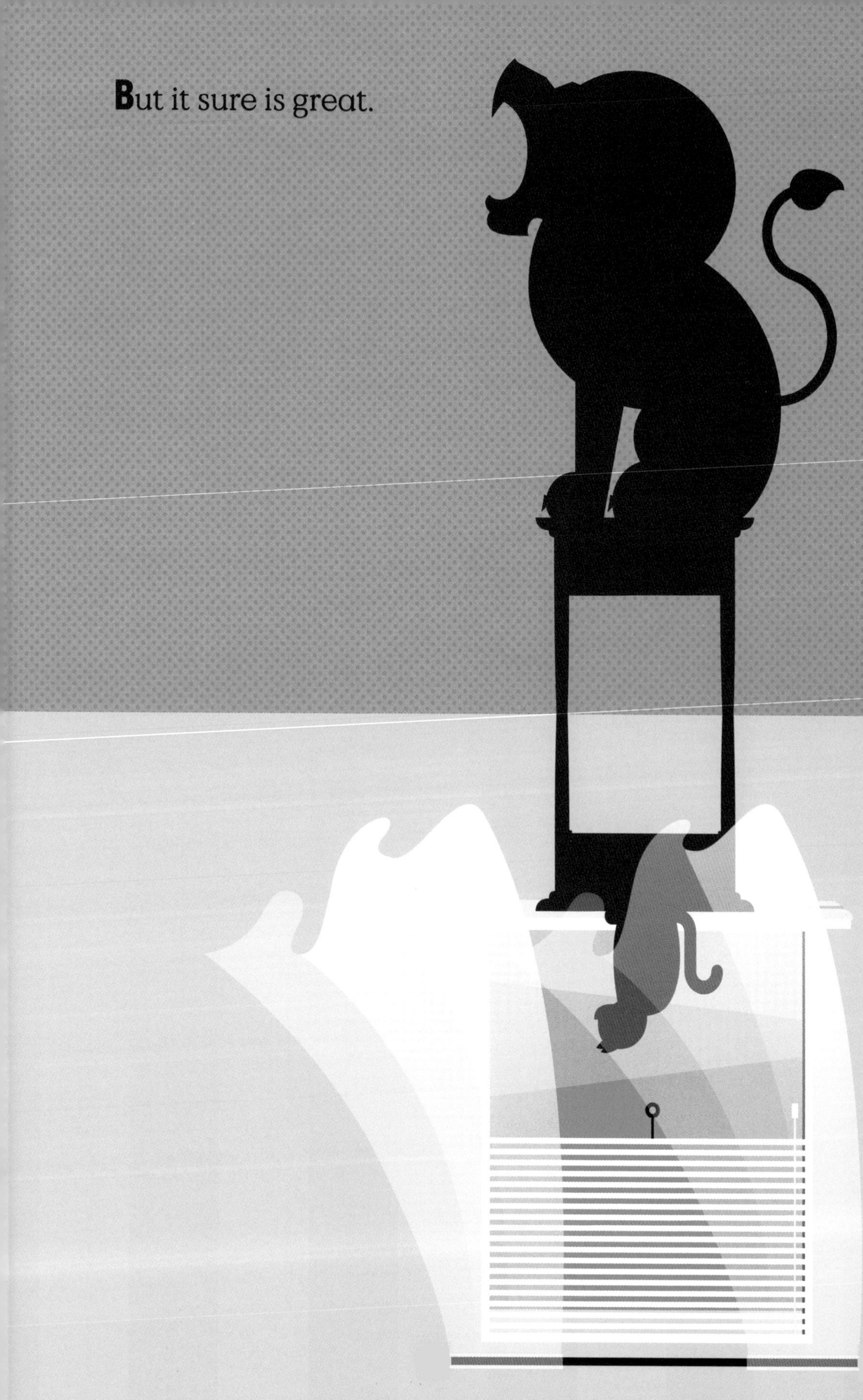

Some days are a three-ring circus.

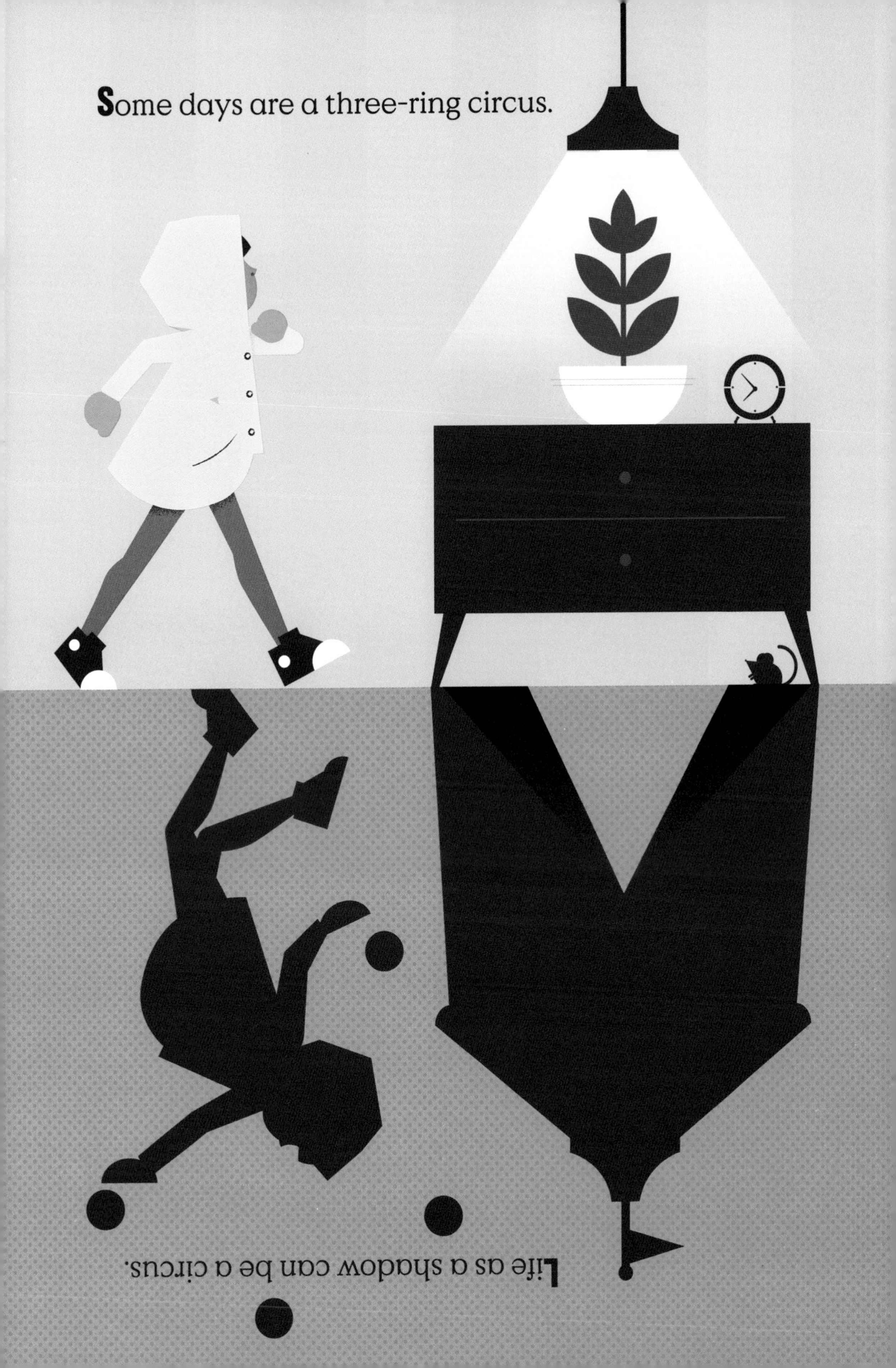

Life as a shadow can be a circus.

I don't usually mind,
but I think my cat does.

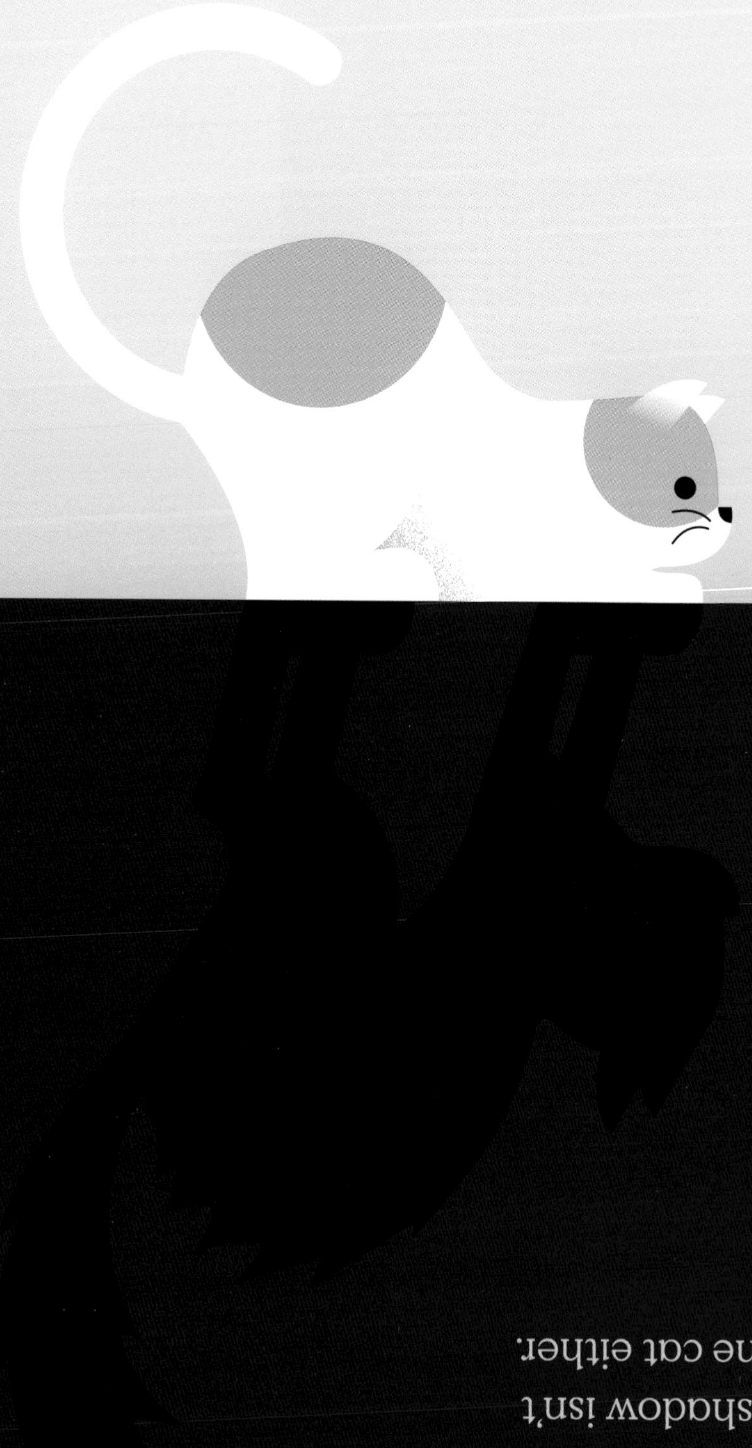

Having a shadow isn't
easy for the cat either.

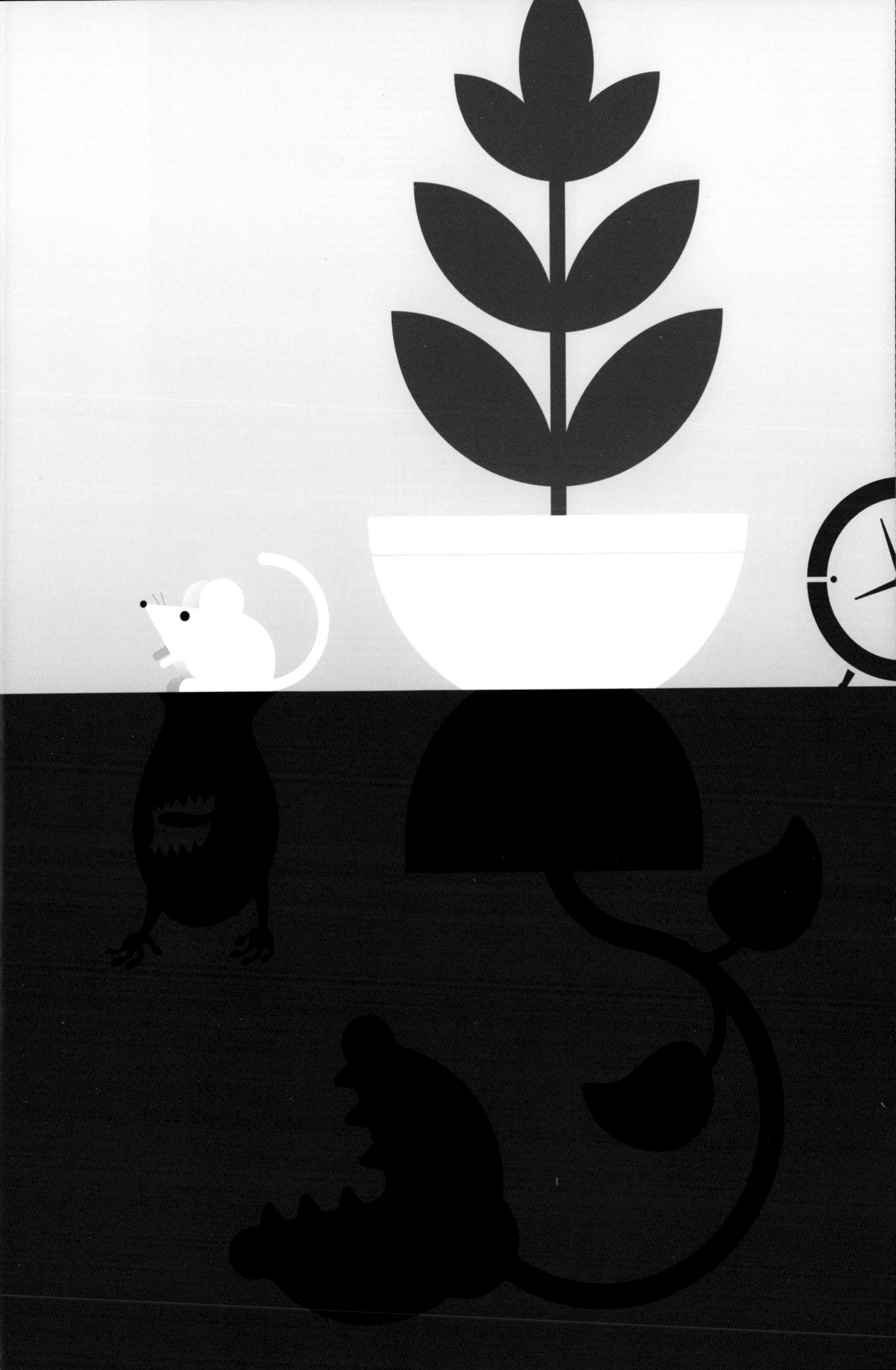

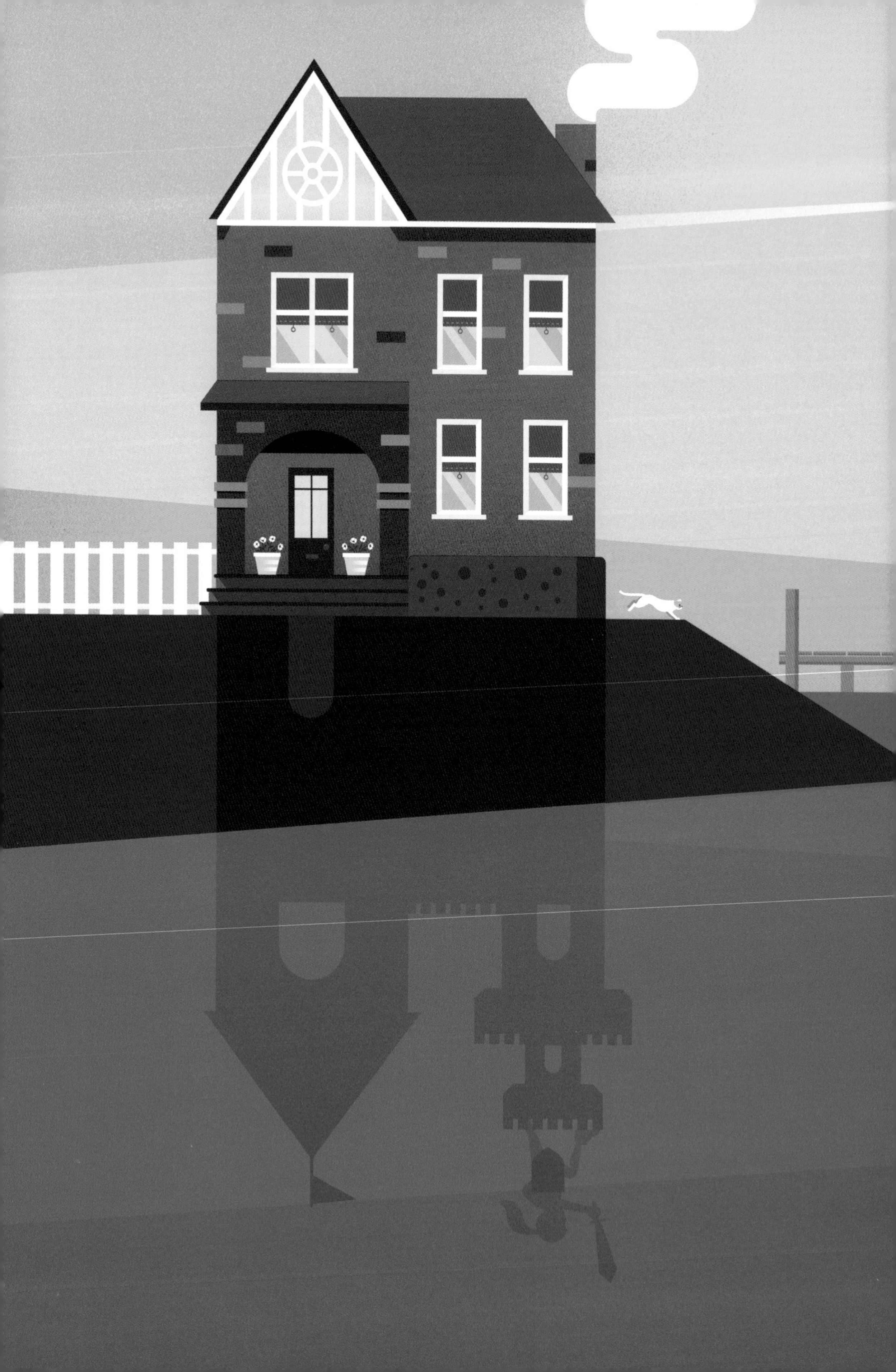

Wherever I go, my shadow follows.

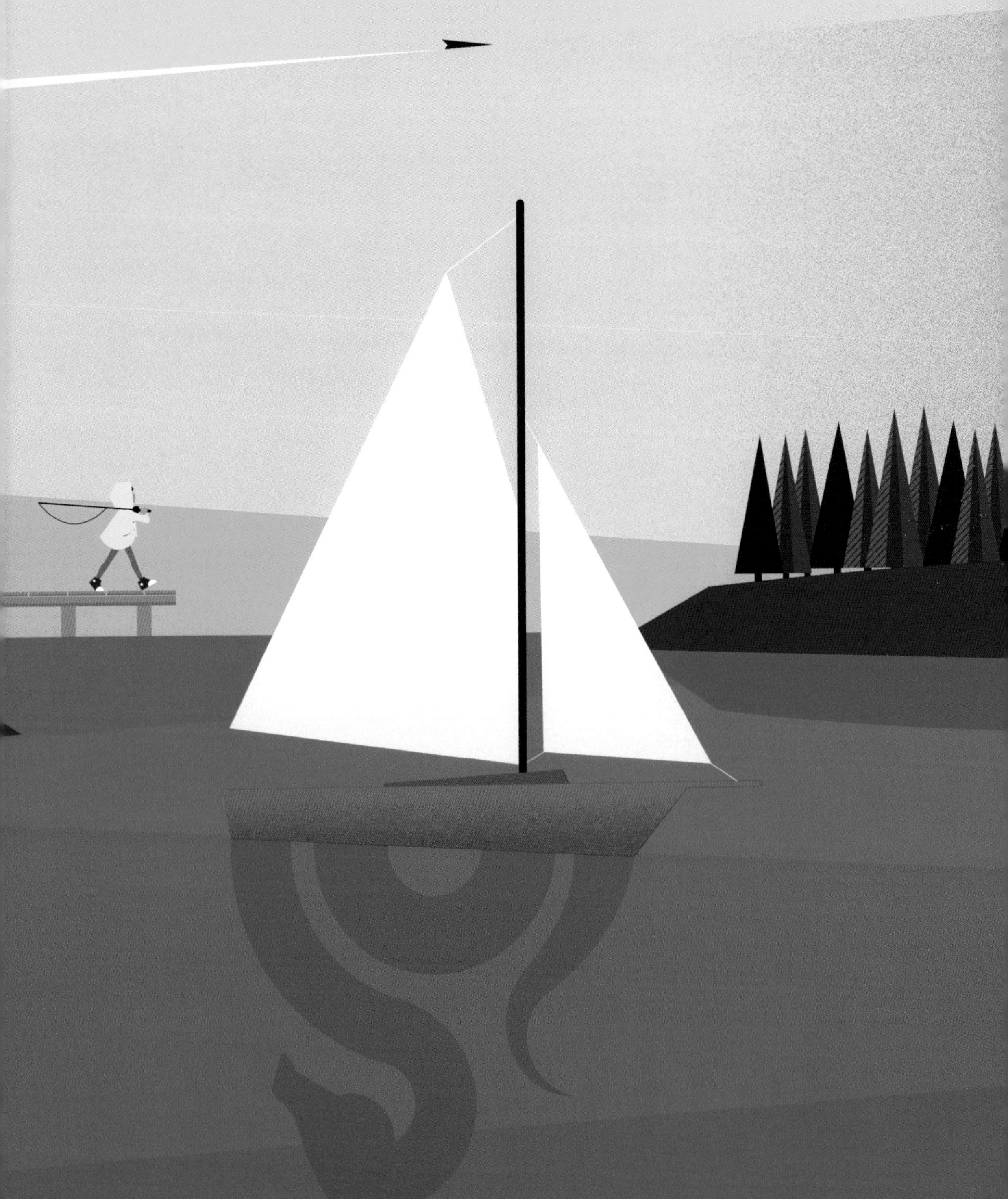

And I take care of any monsters
lurking in the shadows.

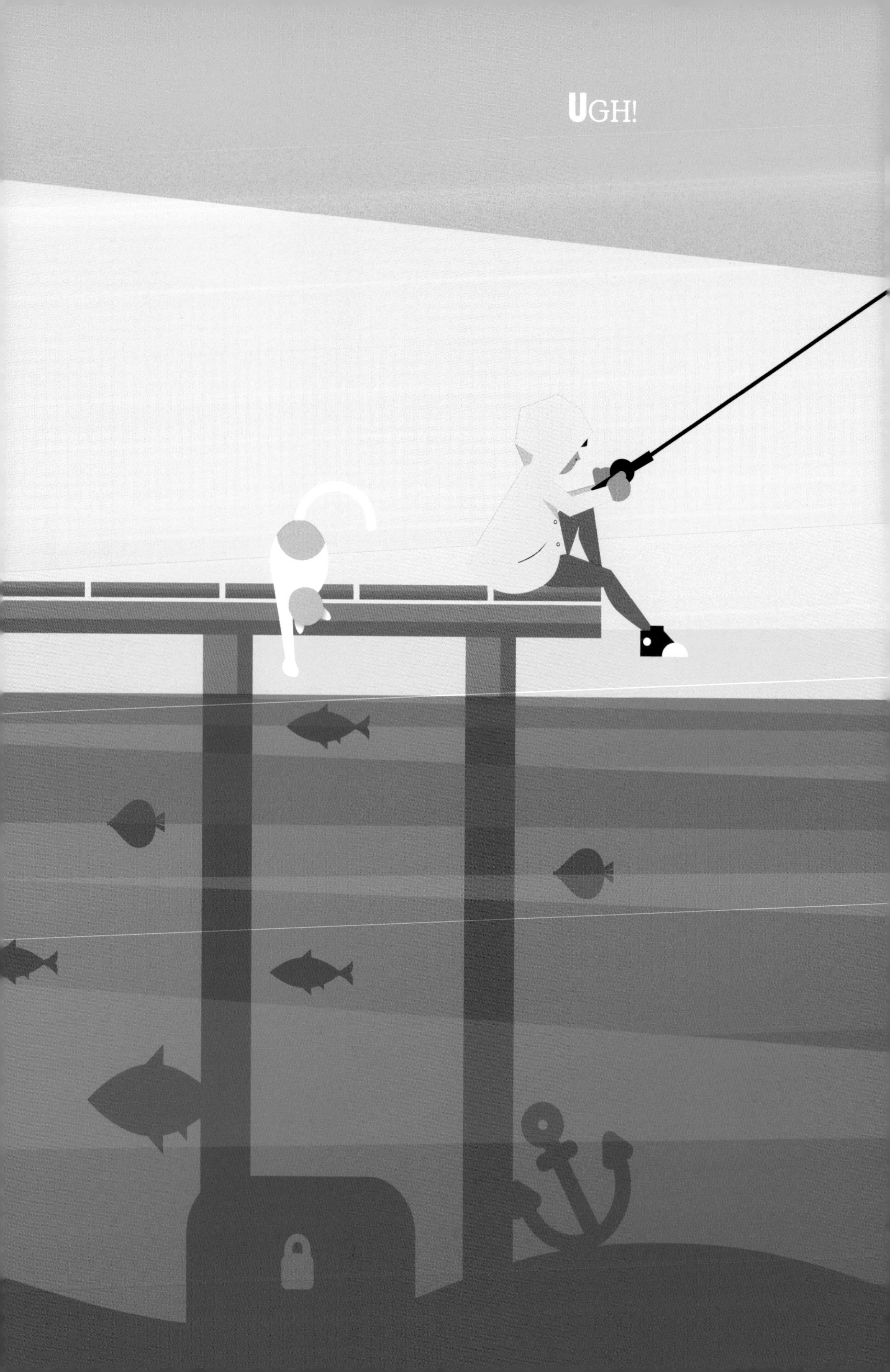
UGH!

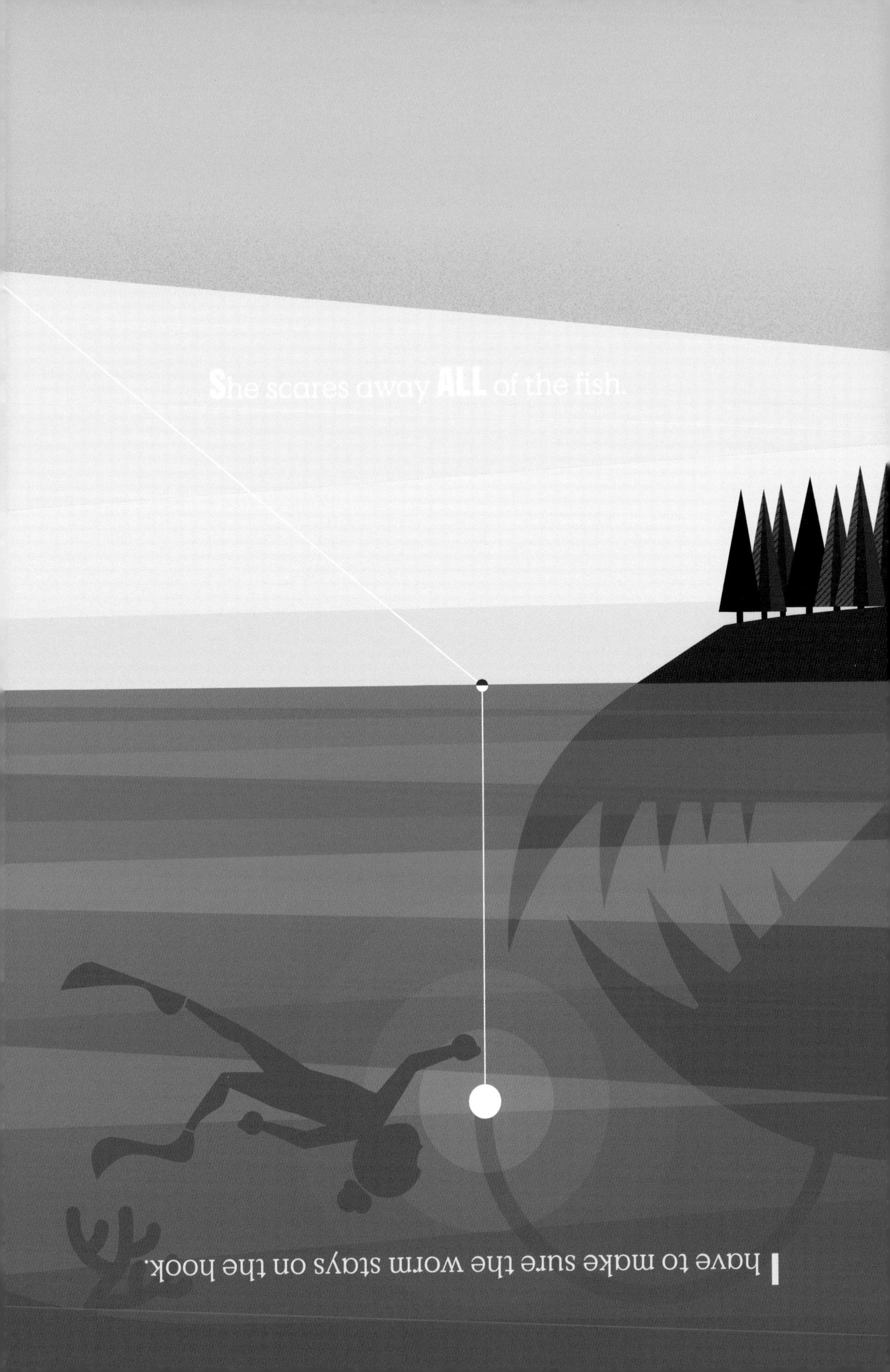

She scares away **ALL** of the fish.

I have to make sure the worm stays on the hook.

Not to mention, she brings along the creepies.

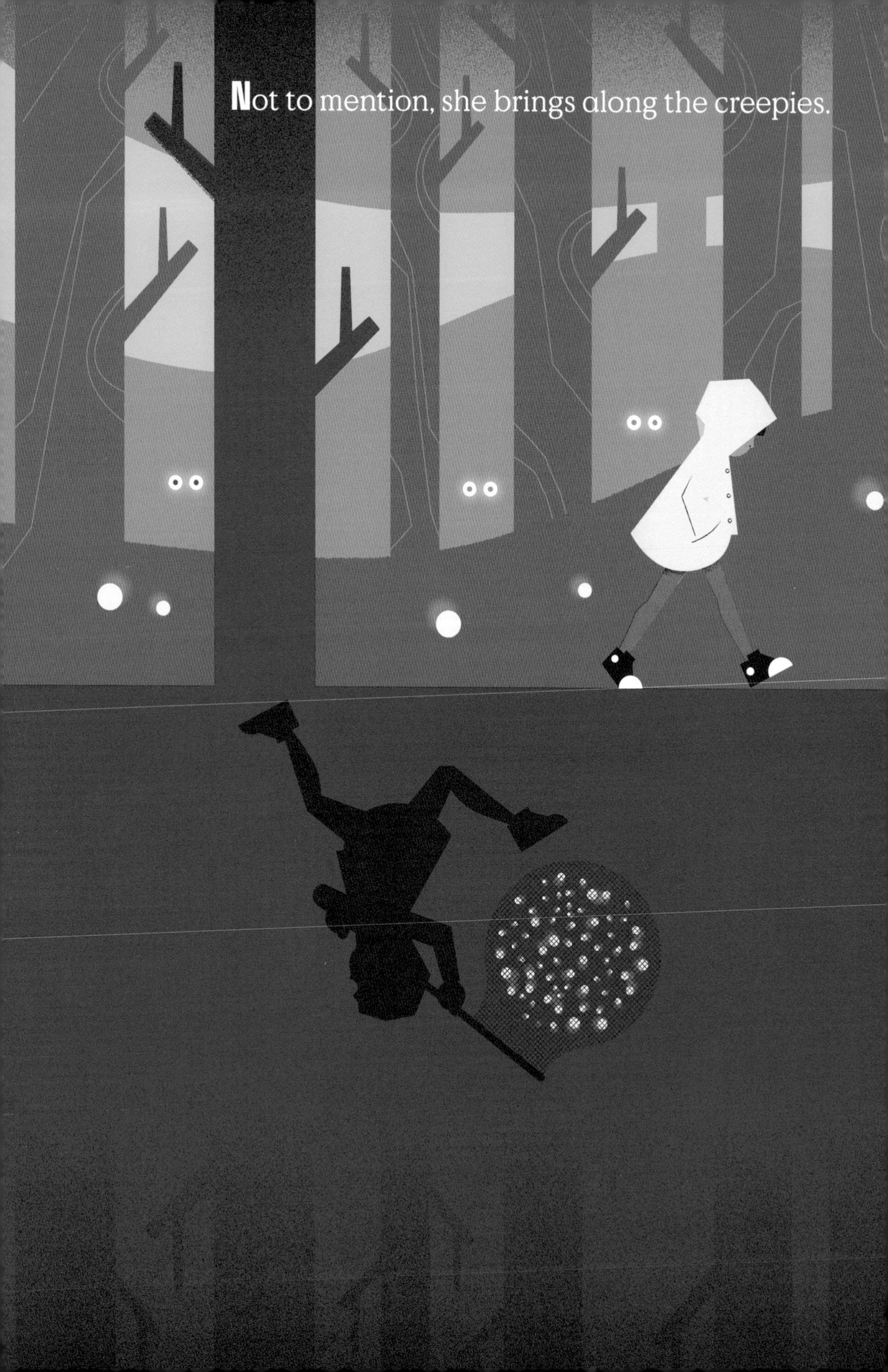

I keep away the creepies.

She even tries to pet the zoo animals.

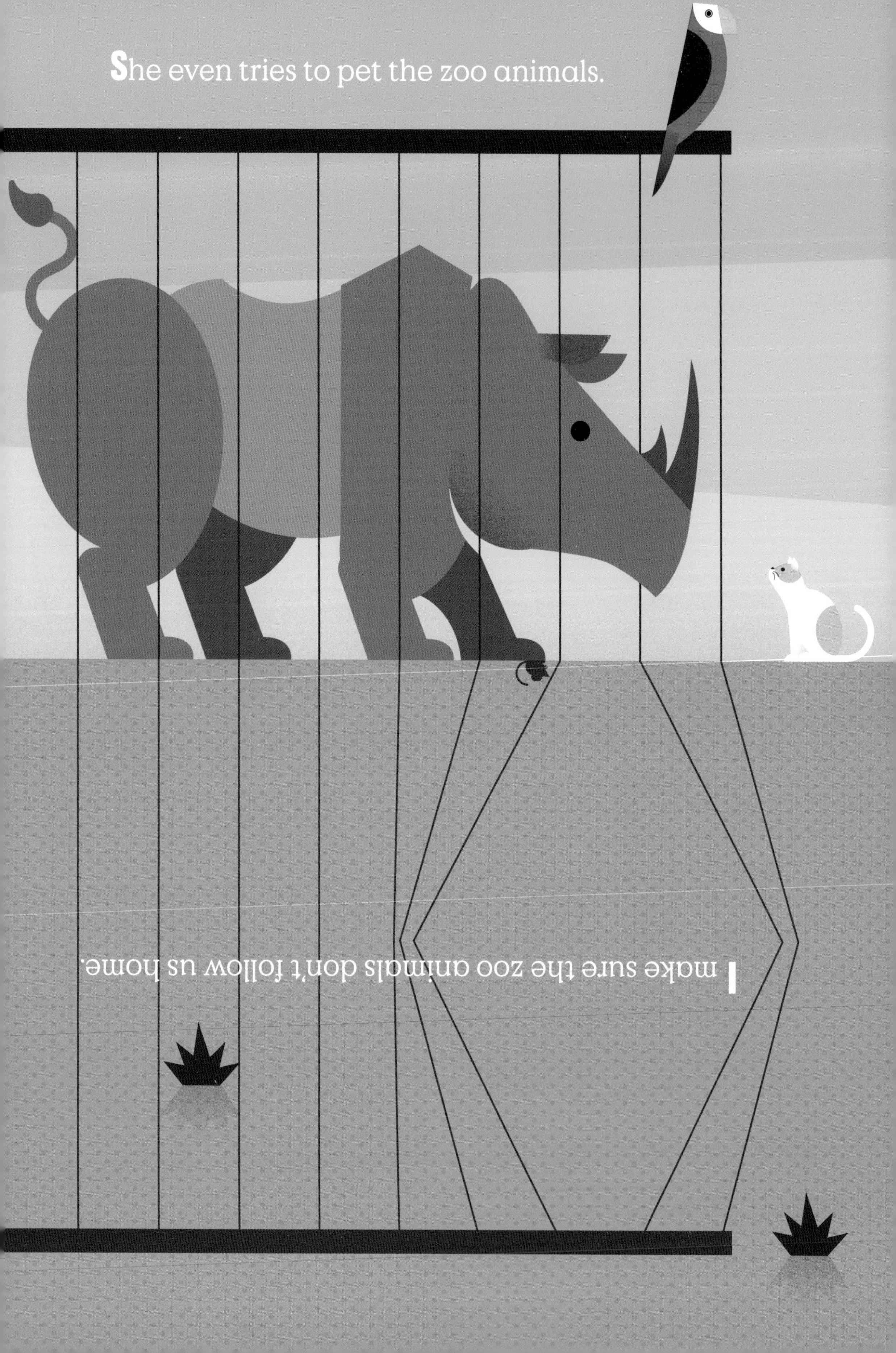

I make sure the zoo animals don't follow us home.

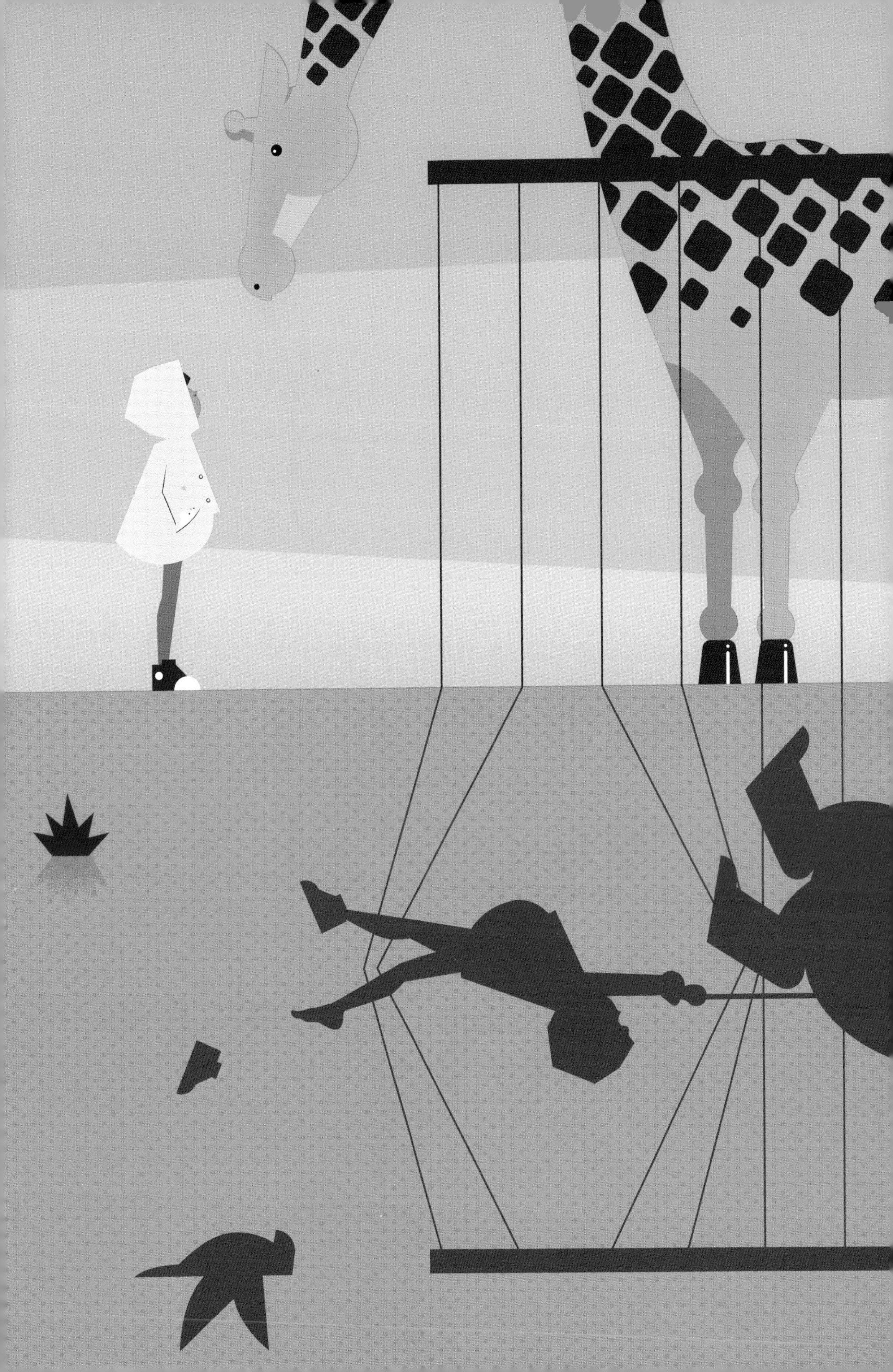

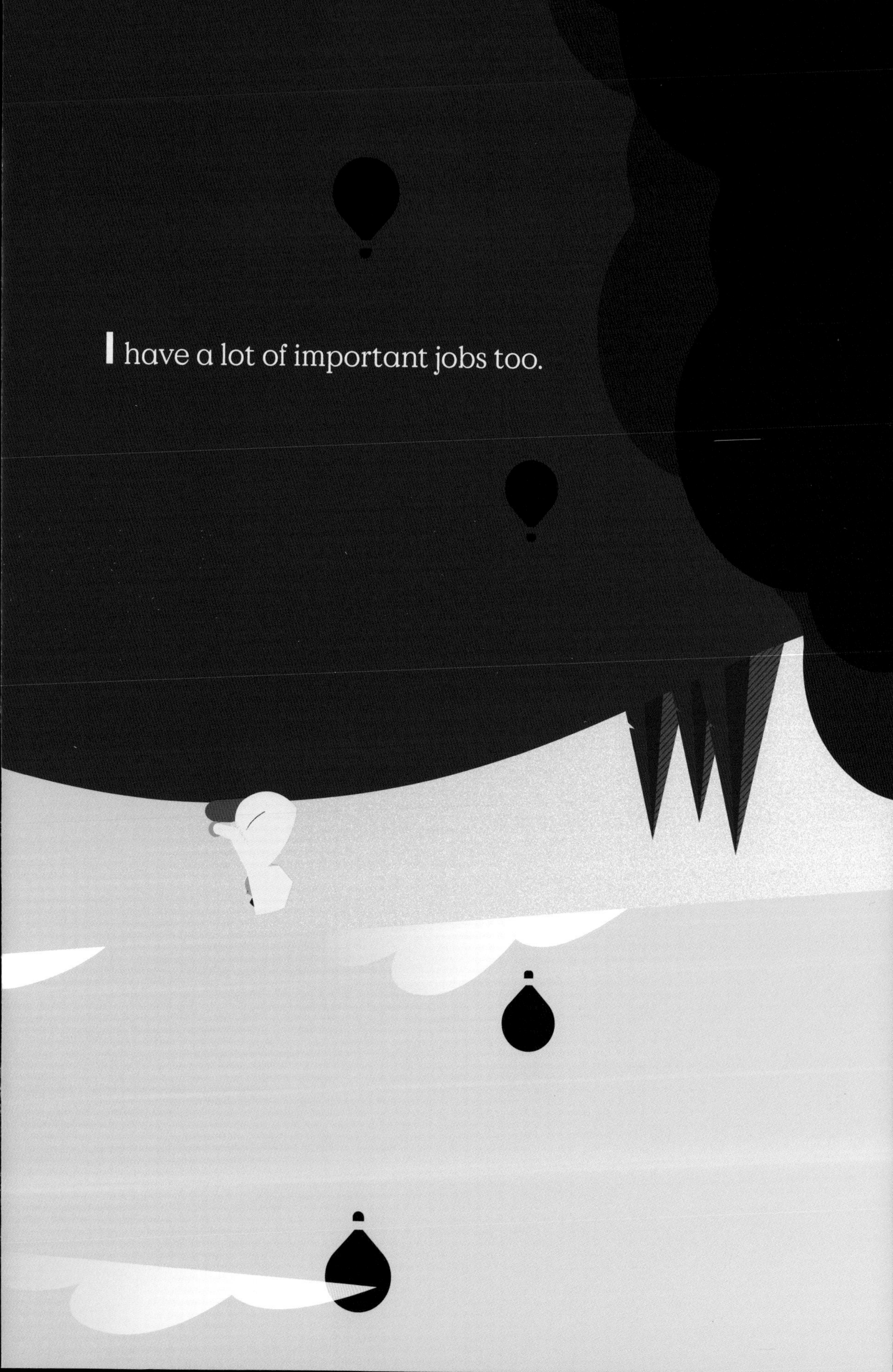

I have a lot of important jobs too.

Some days I think it would be nice to be alone.

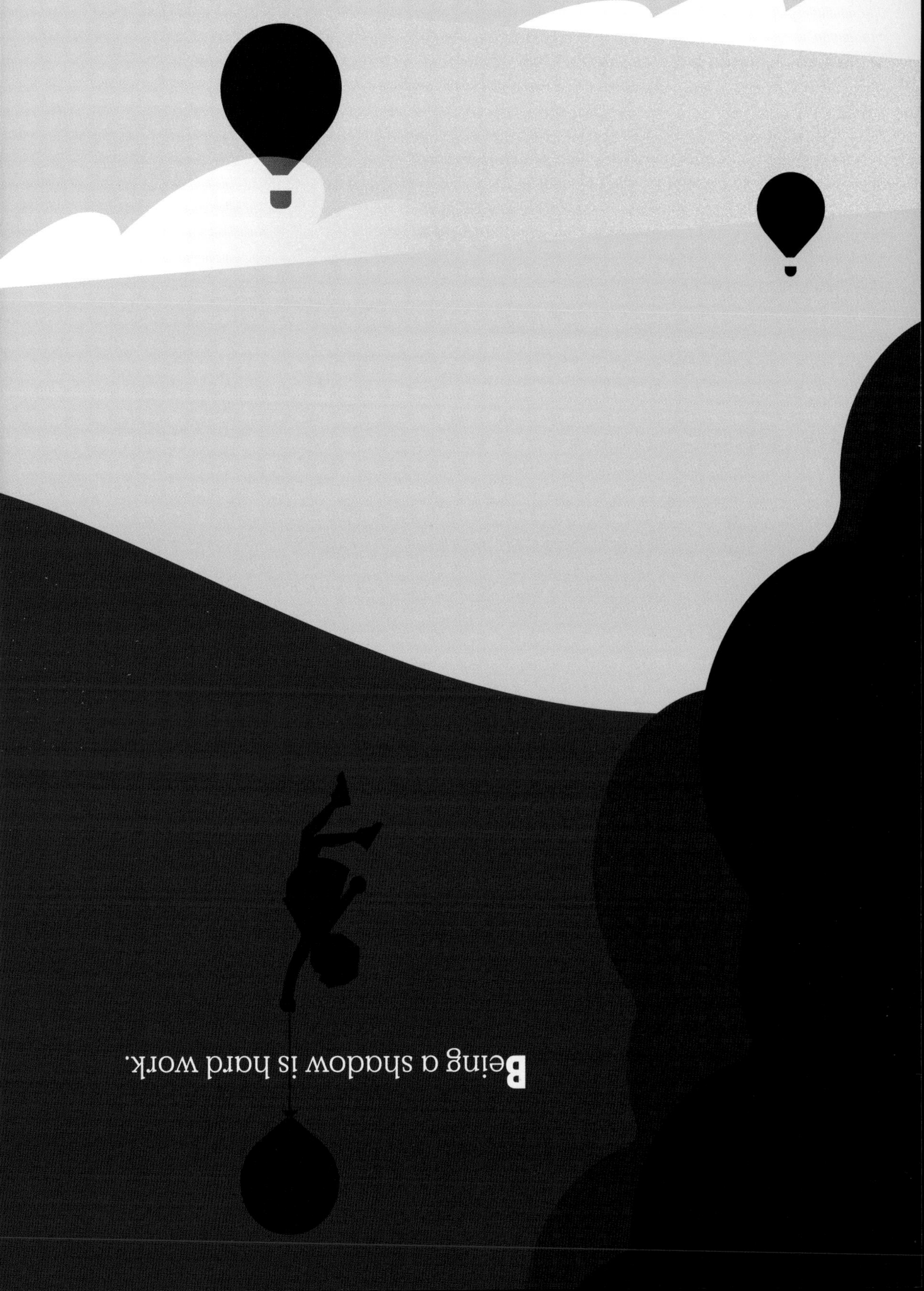

Being a shadow is hard work.

How do you get rid of a shadow that will **NOT** disappear?

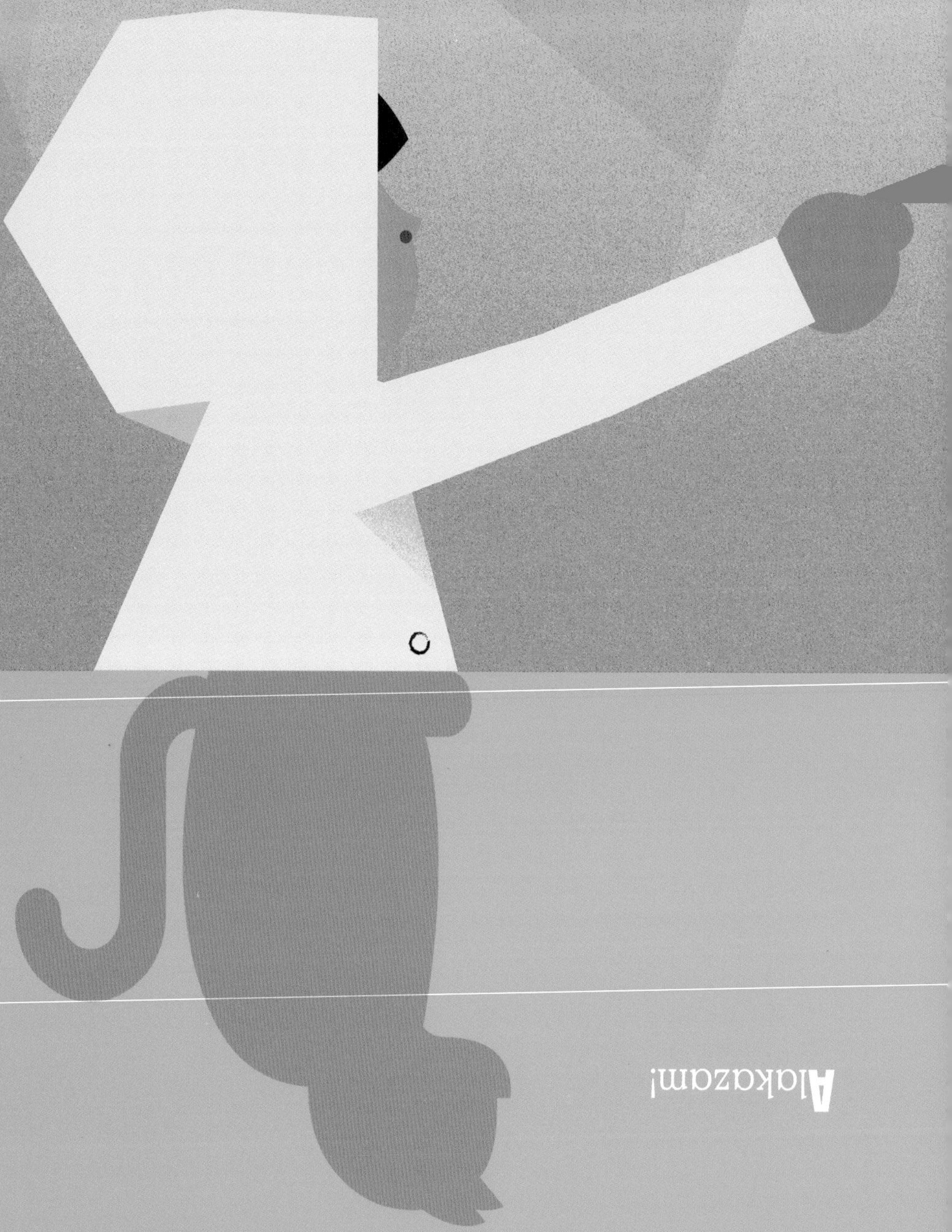

Alakazam!

Abracadabra!

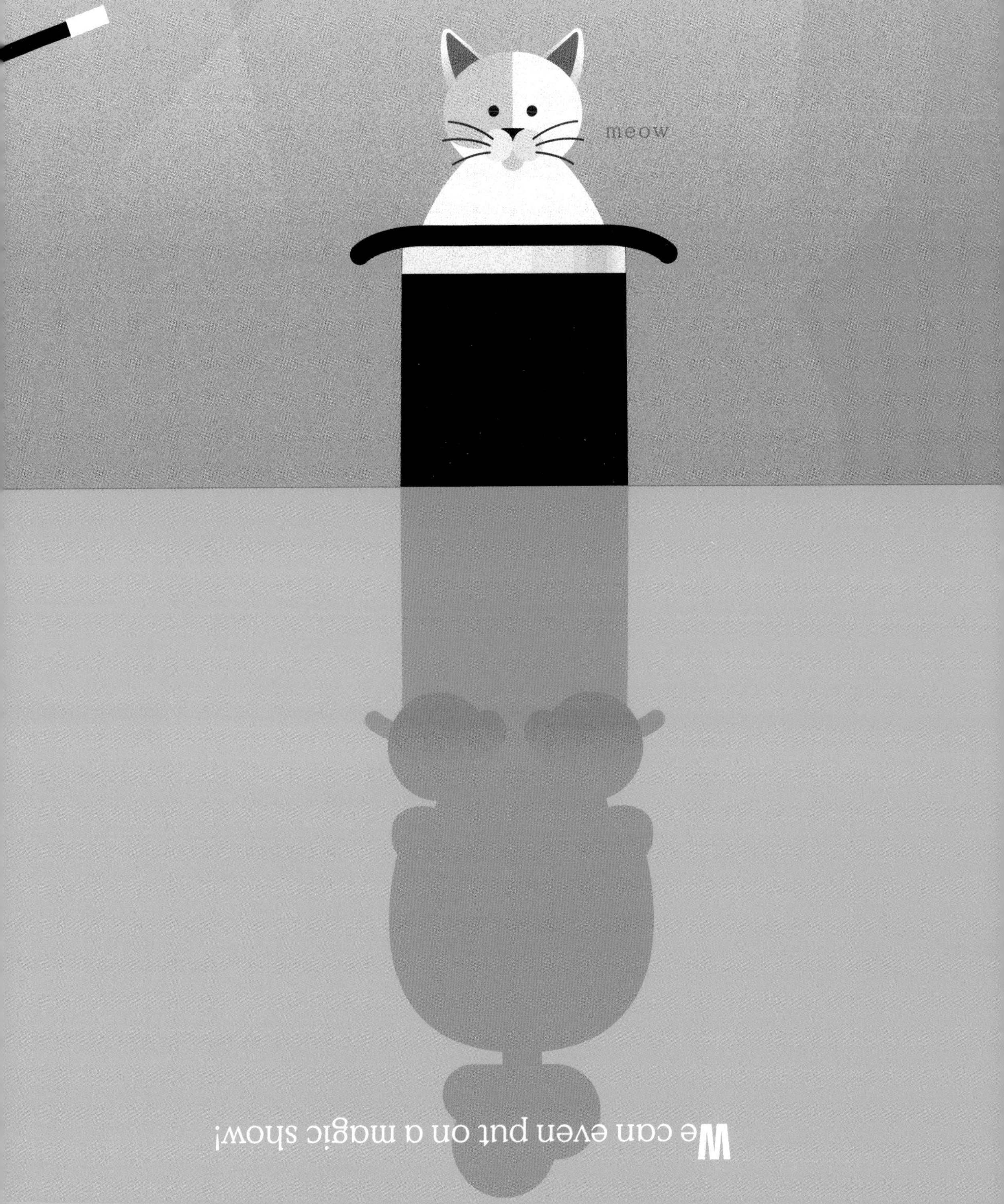

meow

We can even put on a magic show!

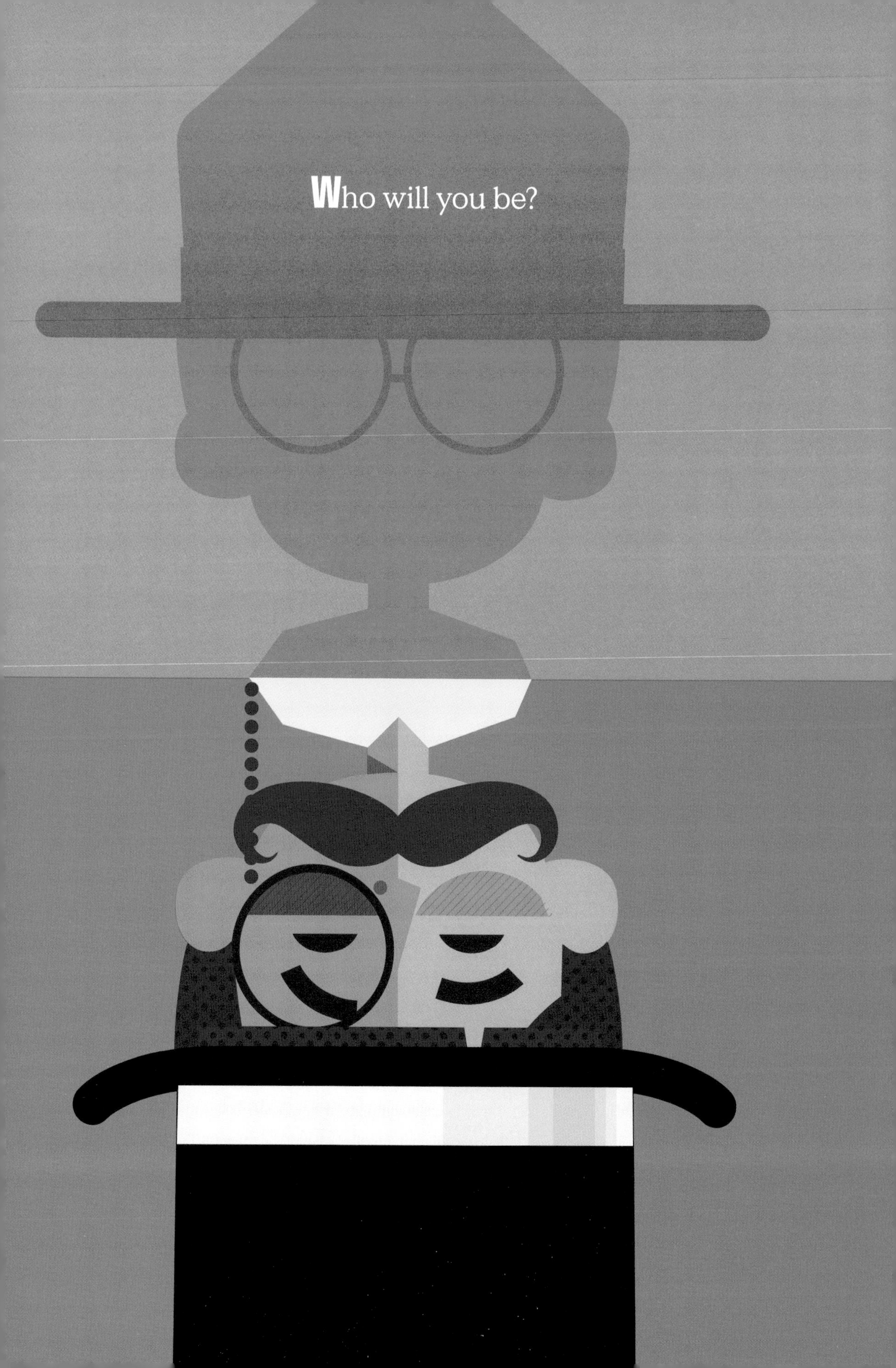
Who will you be?

I can wear a disguise.

good day to you!

We can play dress-up.

Or distract her and run far, far, far away.

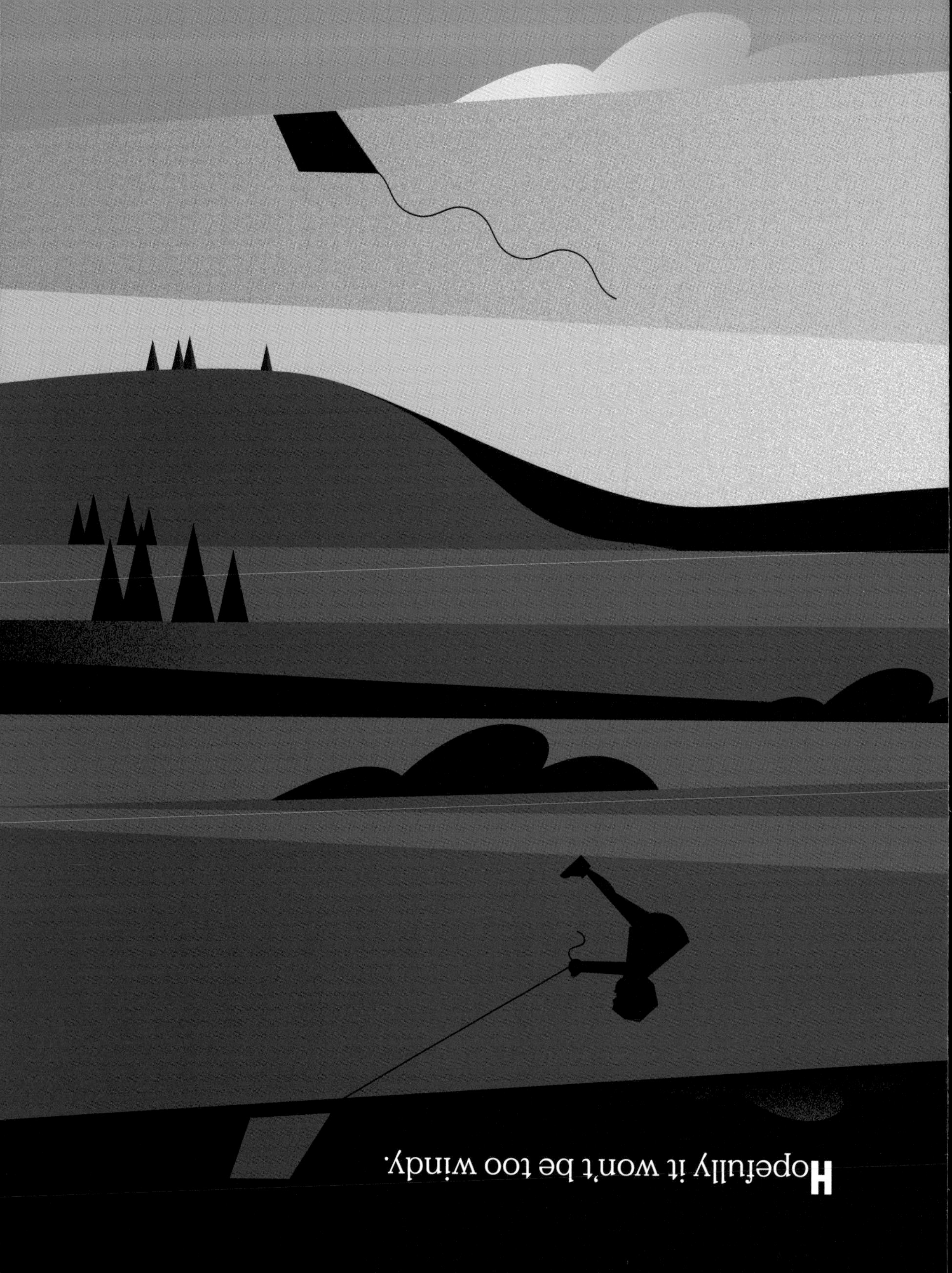

Hopefully it won't be too windy.

We can fly our kites.

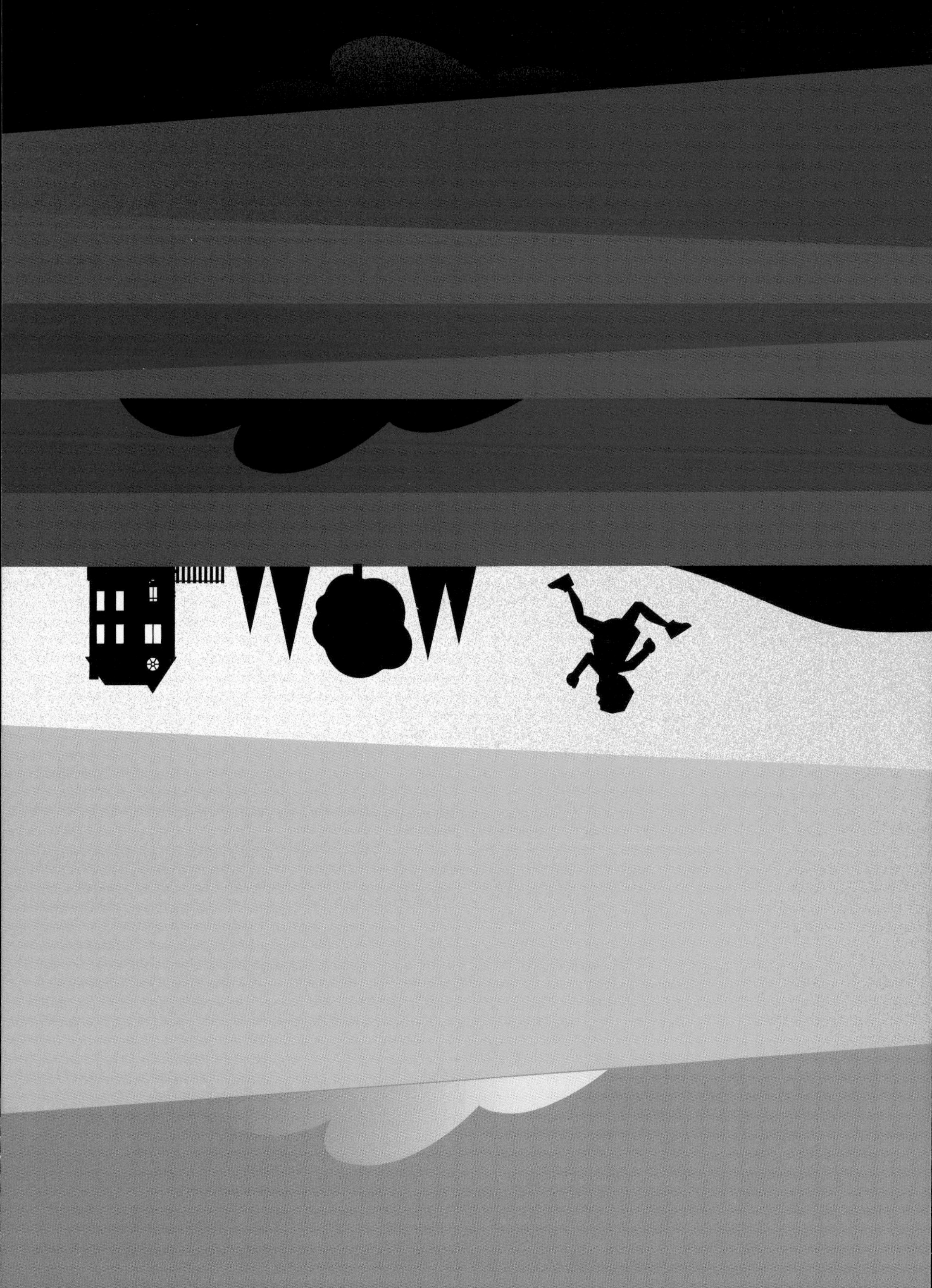

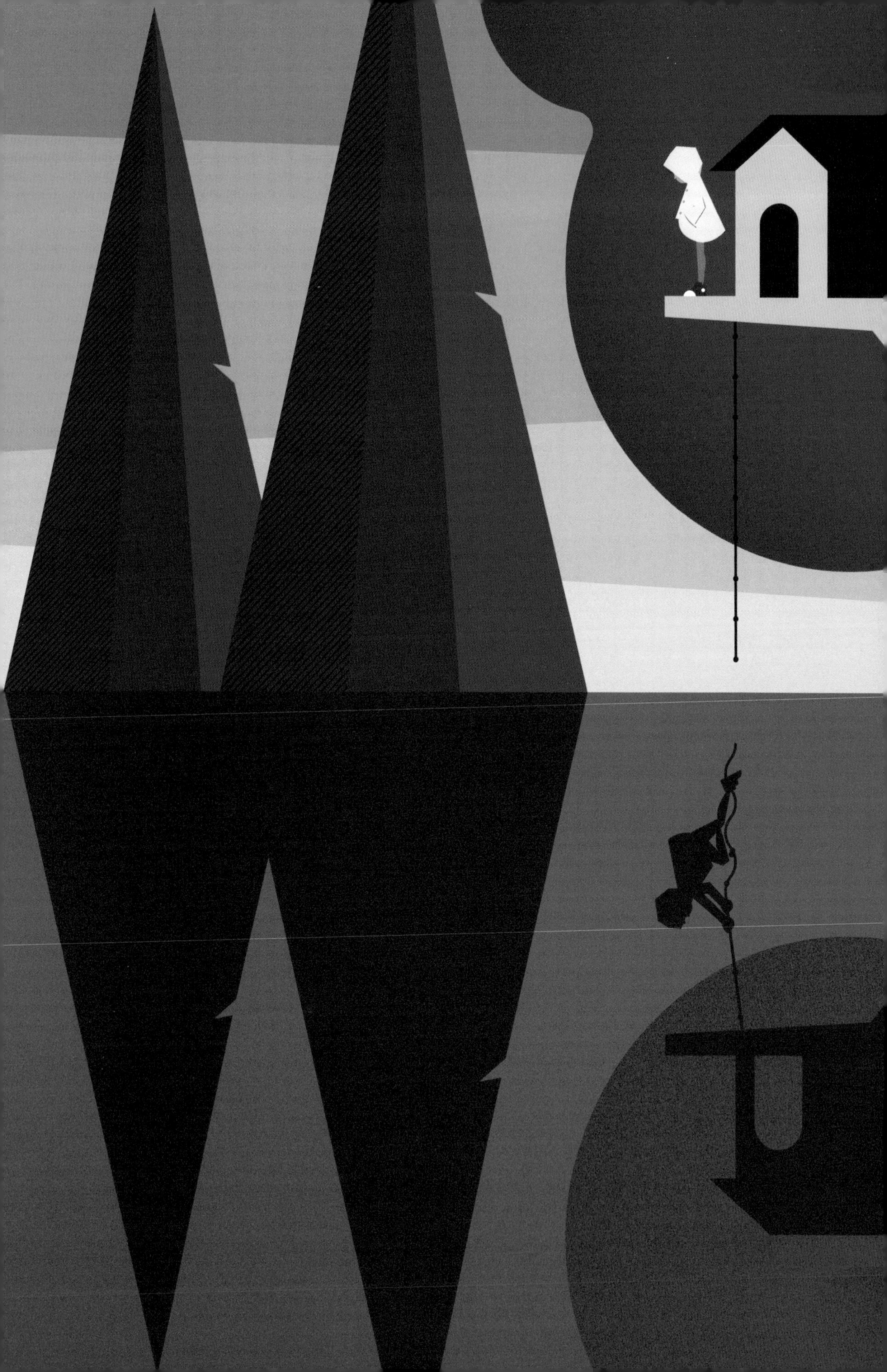

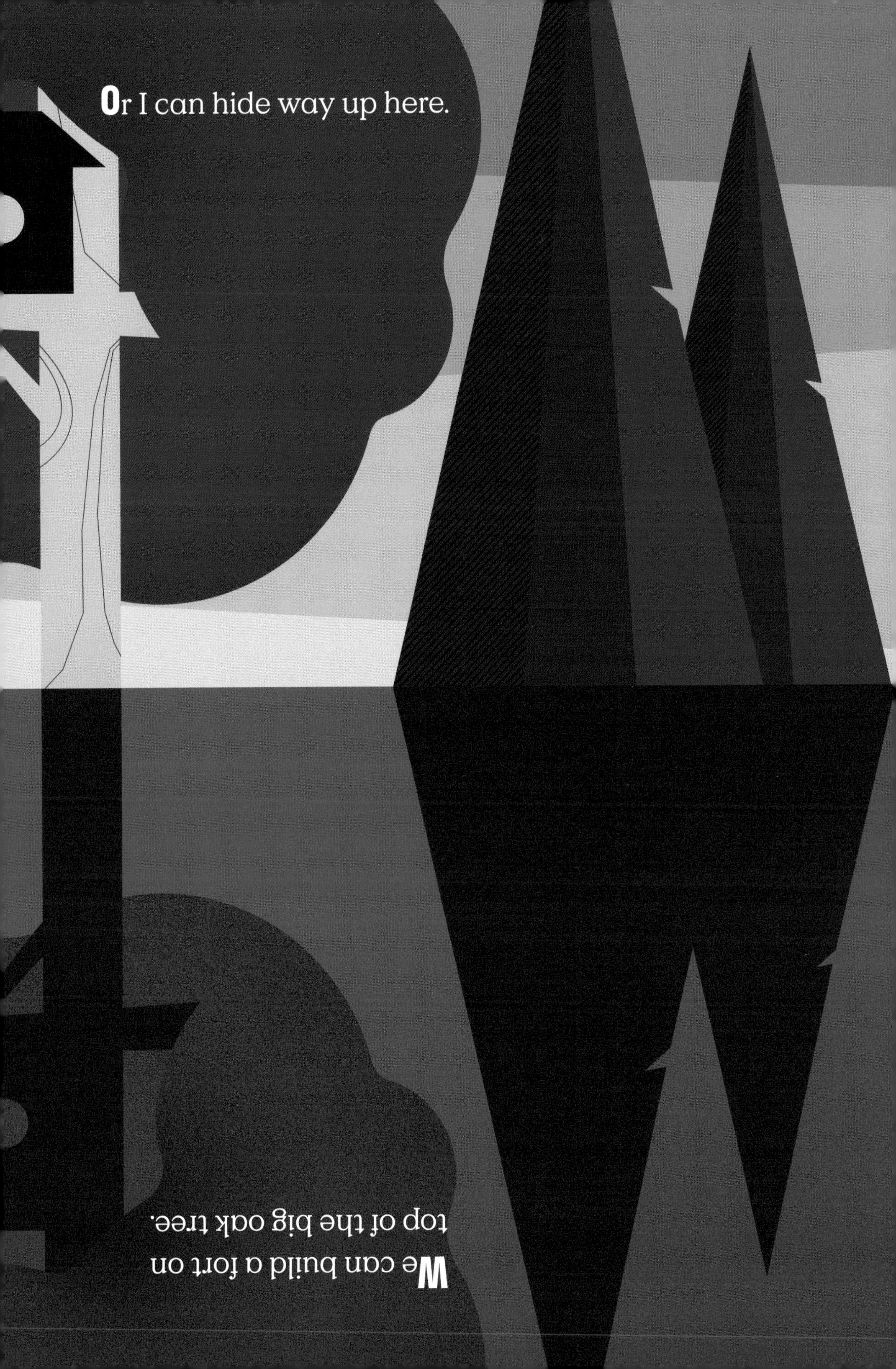

Or I can hide way up here.

We can build a fort on top of the big oak tree.

There is so much to do. Tag. You're it!

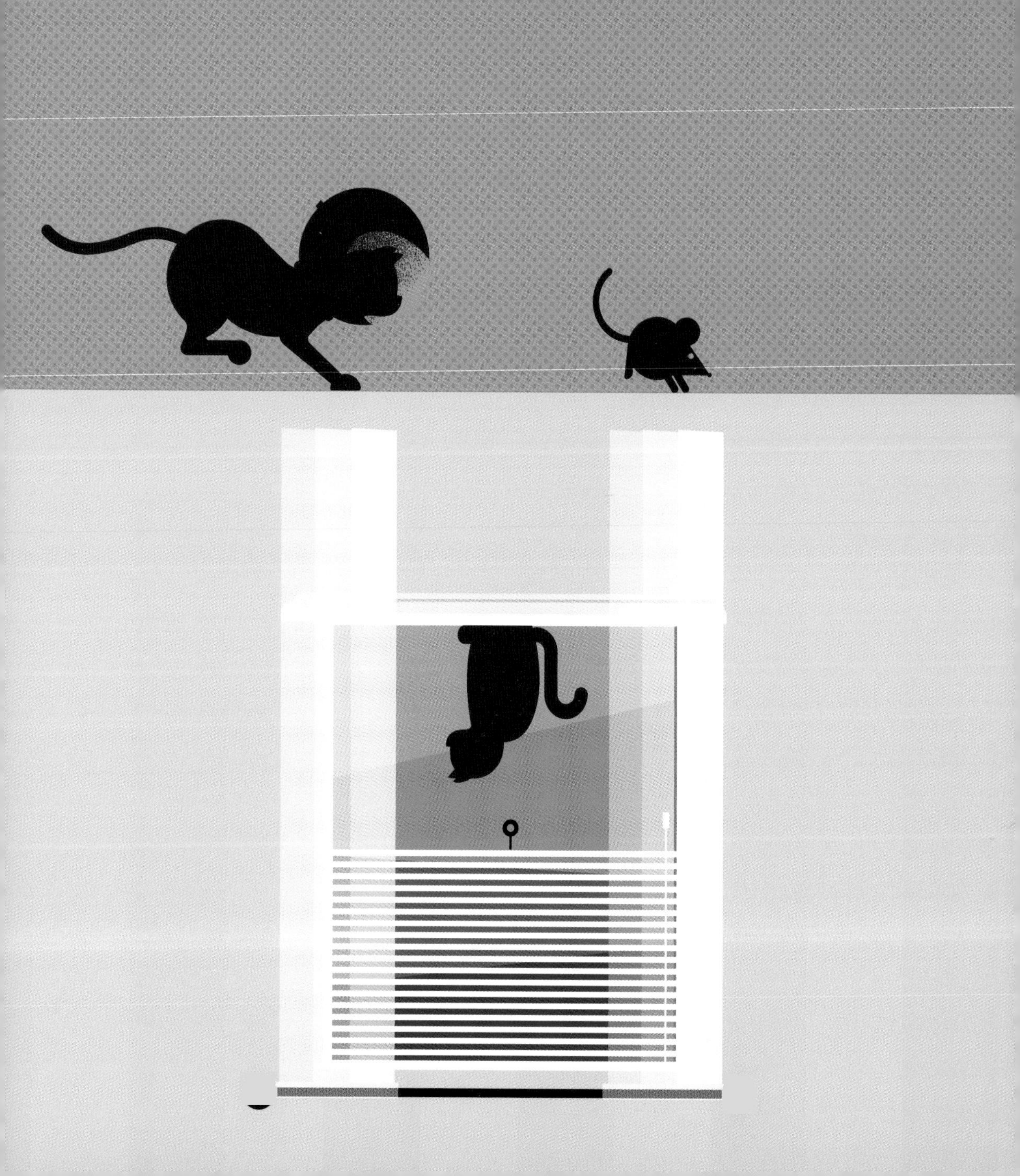

There is only one true way to get rid of an annoying, irritating, always-in-the-way shadow.

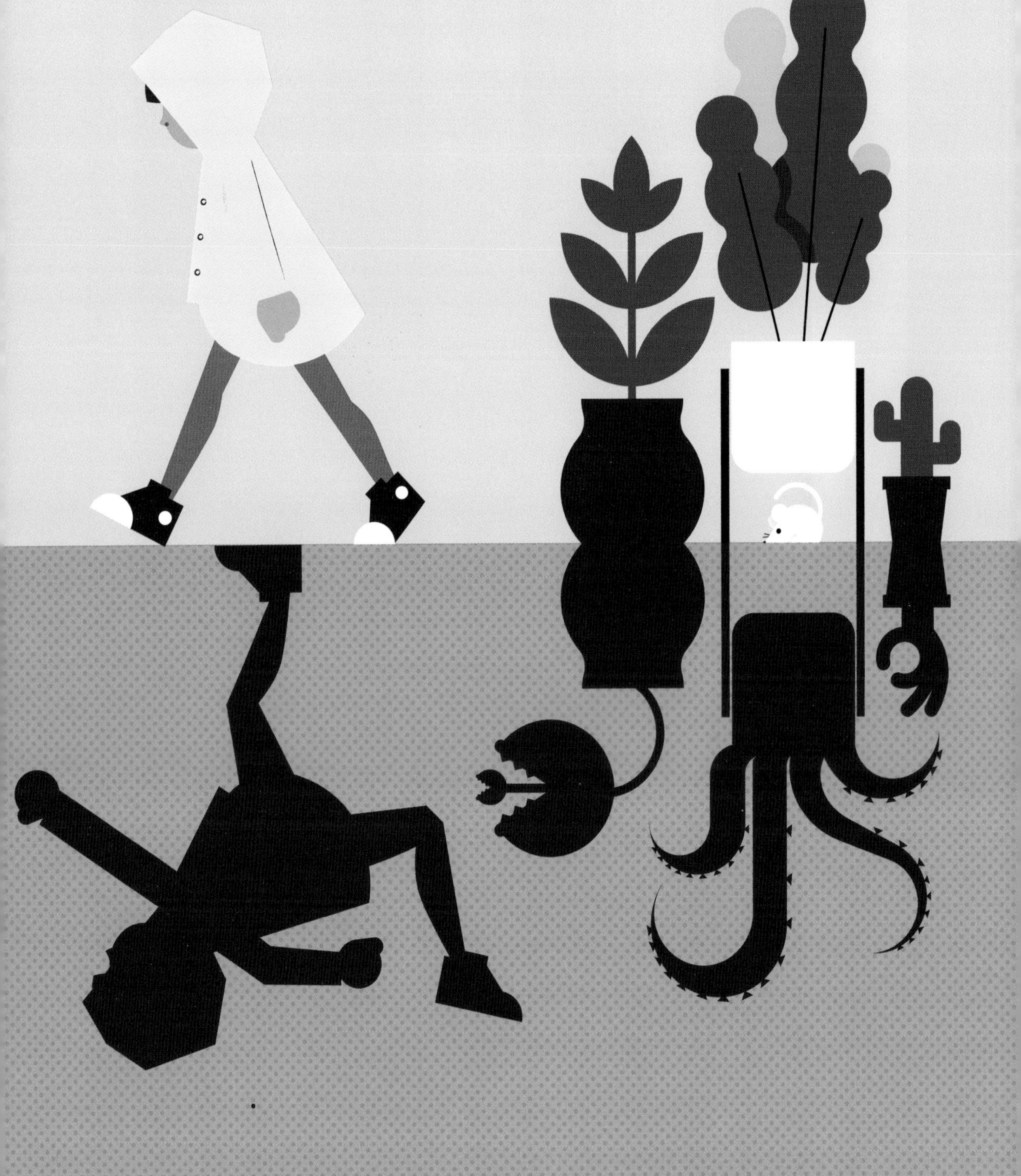

I hope you are ready to play!

Your daring, dashing, always-up-for-an-adventure shadow is ready for the new day!

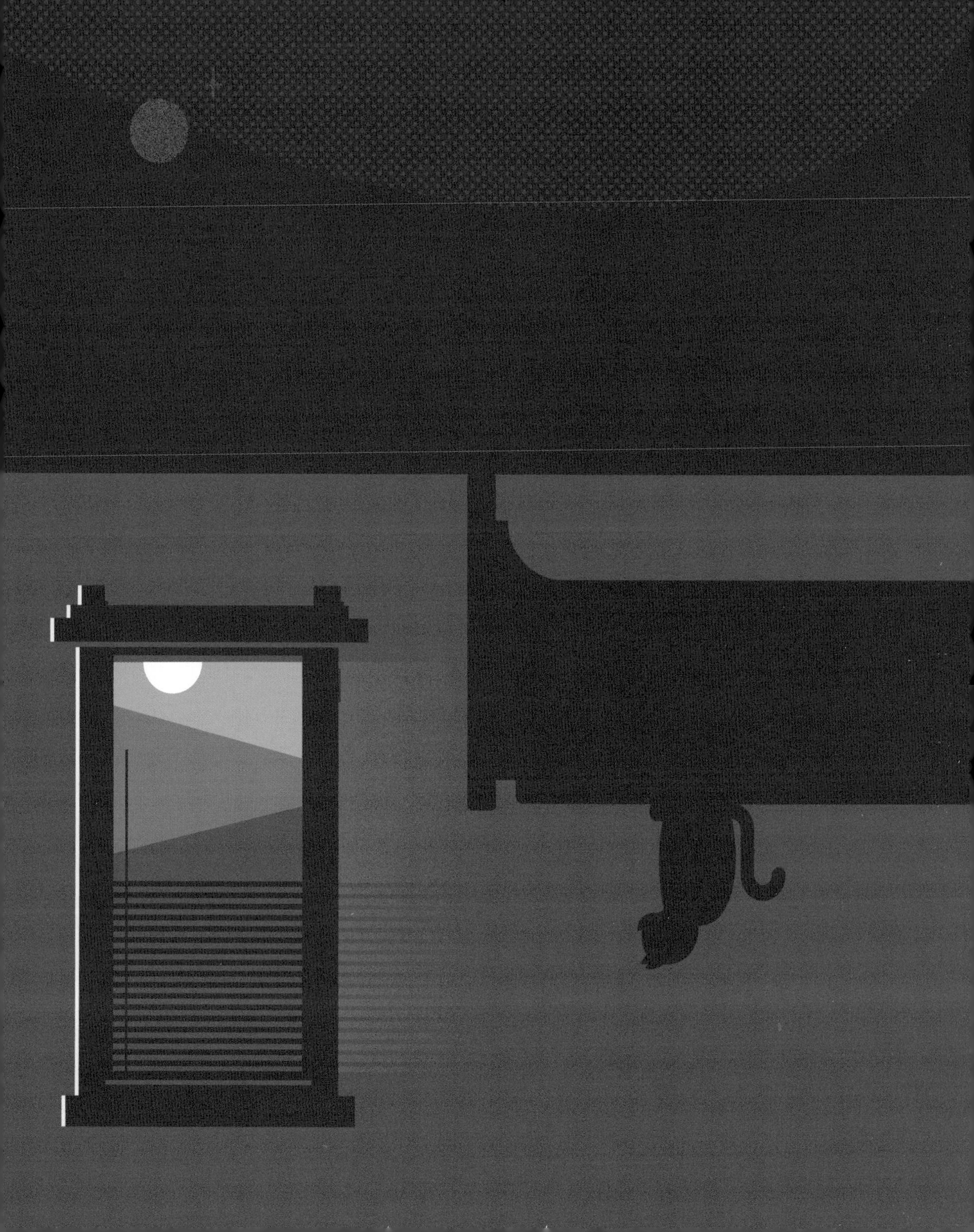

Turn out the lights!

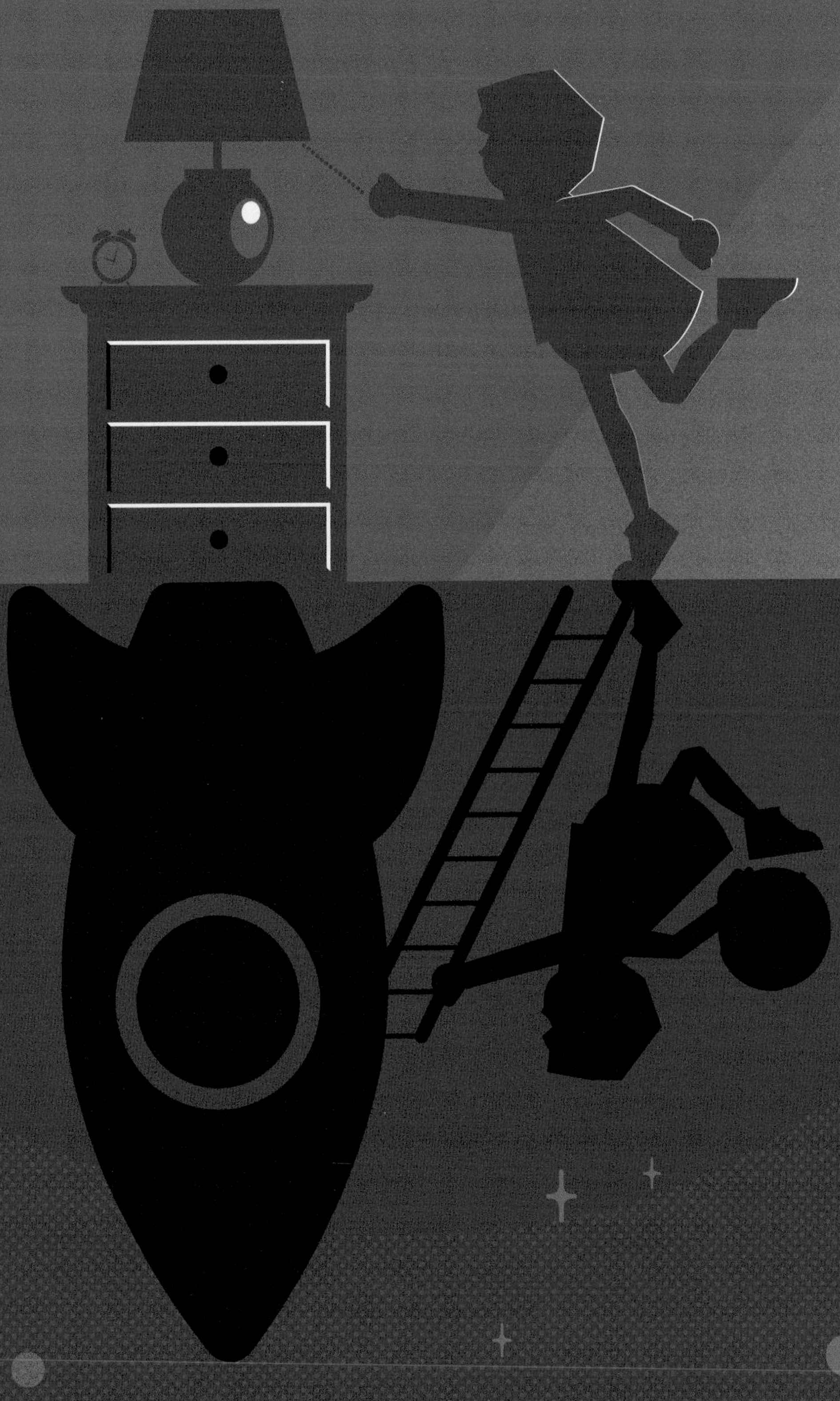

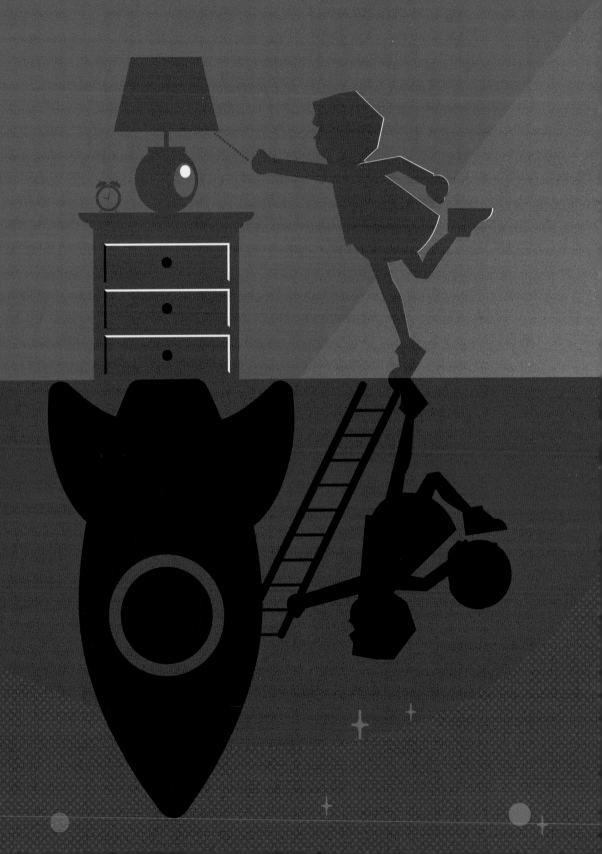

zzzzzzzZ

That means...

Wait, wait! I'm almost there. The stars are fading,
and soon the sun will rise.

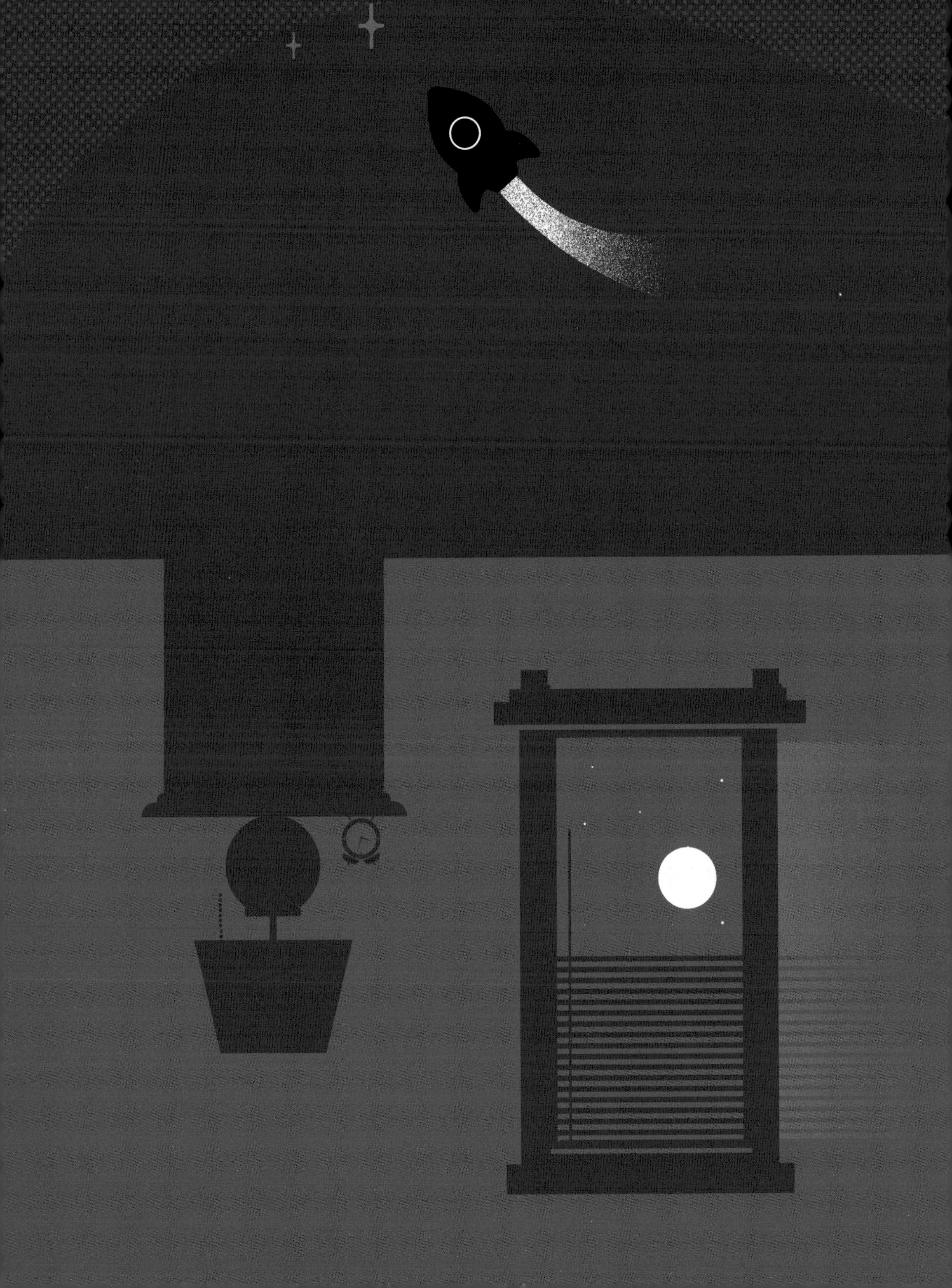

Turn this book around and read another story.